"Would you like to hear a
Mrs. Bear asked Bo.
"I'm too big for lullabies," Bo replied and
headed off to bed.

Bo tossed and turned. "There must be something wrong with my bed," he thought. And then he looked under the pillow. . .

"I wonder if Buster is sleeping—
his bed is always so crowded..."

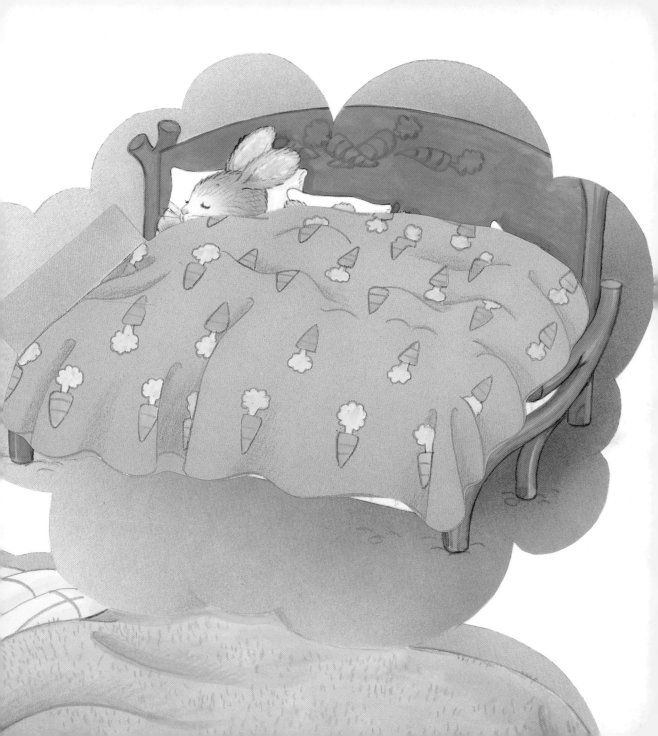

And Bo wondered if Dixie floated on the water when she went to sleep.

"Dot's bed must be really cozy, but tiny," Bo thought to himself.

But in his own bed Bo still couldn't fall asleep.
Tall shadows on the wall were giving him the creeps!

Perhaps sleeping with his new toy doggie would help.

It didn't! Then Bo heard a strange sound outside the window.

"Maybe a glass of milk will help you sleep," Mom suggested.

The milk was very tasty, but it didn't help Bo sleep.
"Mom, will you read me a story?" Bo asked with a sigh.
"Sure," Mrs. Bear replied, "right after I sing Daddy
a lullaby."